EVERY DAY BIRDS

BY Amy Ludwig VanDerwater

CUT PAPER ILLUSTRATIONS BY
Dylan Metrano

ORCHARD BOOKS / NEW YORK / AN IMPRINT OF SCHOLASTIC INC.

Every day we watch for birds
weaving through our sky.

We listen to their calls and songs.

We like to see them fly.

CHICKADEE

wears a wee

black cap.

JAY

is loud and bold.

NUTHATCH

perches

upside-down.

FiNCH

is clothed

in gold.

HAWK

hunts

every

day

for

prey.

CARDiNAL

flashes

fire.

WOODPECKER

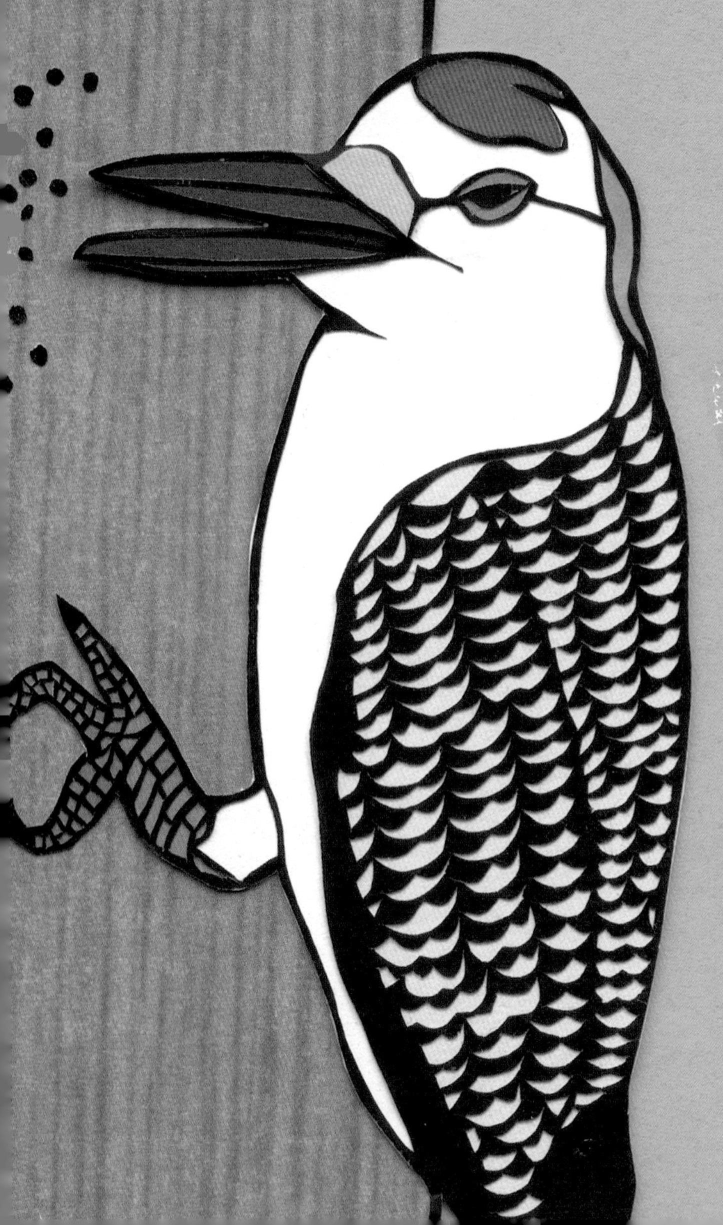

taps

hollow

trees.

CROW

rests on a wire.

fishes with his bill.

SPARROW

hops in brown.

has many voices.

PIGEON

lives in town.

EAGLE

soars

above

the

land.

ORiOLe

hangs

her

nest.

OWL swoops soundlessly

late

at

night.

ROBiN

puffs

his

chest.

HUMMiNGBiRD

drinks flower nectar.

GOOSE
flies in a V.

BLUEBIRD

sleeps at

meadow's

edge.

GULL

stares at the sea.

Every day we watch for birds
living right outside our door.

We pay attention to the birds.
Every day we learn some more.

Every day we watch for birds
weaving through our sky.
We listen to their calls and songs.
We like to see them fly.
Chickadee wears a wee black cap.
Jay is loud and bold.
Nuthatch perches upside-down.
Finch is clothed in gold.

Hawk hunts every day for prey.
Cardinal flashes fire.
Woodpecker taps hollow trees.
Crow rests on a wire.
Heron fishes with his bill.
Sparrow hops in brown.
Mockingbird has many voices.
Pigeon lives in town.

Eagle soars above the land.

Oriole hangs her nest.

Owl swoops soundlessly late at night.

Robin puffs his chest.

Hummingbird drinks flower nectar.

Goose flies in a V.

Bluebird sleeps at meadow's edge.

Gull stares at the sea.

Every day we watch for birds

living right outside our door.

We pay attention to the birds.

Every day we learn some more.

EVERY DAY, BIRDS ADD A LAYER OF BEAUTY AND INTEREST TO OUR LIVES.

Each day offers new treasures, right outside of any home, classroom, or office window. In city streets, on cul-de-sacs, peppering country skies, birds are here: flashing wings, singing songs, making nests from bits and scraps they find. We can watch and learn new birds, and we can get to know old friends, too. We can keep lists of birds we have seen, and we can talk about birds with friends. We can sketch birds and we can read books about them. Every day, there are endless ways to enjoy these gifts of color and cleverness.

This book focuses on twenty common North American birds. Using a field guide, you can learn specifics of the birds that live near and fly by your home. There are many feathered creatures to discover, and here is a place to begin. I wish you a lifetime of birds, a lifetime of curiosity!

—AMY

SCIENTIFIC NOTE: Though bluebirds and robins are both thrushes, I felt it was valuable to include each under its more specific name, as they are among the birds that children most quickly and easily identify.

BLUEBIRDS

feed mostly on insects in summer, but in winter they must eat more berries and other wild fruits. They frequently nest in old woodpecker holes and sometimes in boxes built by people. Bluebirds travel in pairs or flocks.

CARDINALS

eat mostly insects in summer and fruit and seeds in winter. They nest in many types of trees and shrubs and do not migrate. Male northern cardinals are famous for their red color, and females are brown.

CHICKADEES eat seeds, often visit bird feeders, and are good at hiding seeds to find in winter. Chickadees build nests in holes in trees. They are curious little birds and will sometimes eat from people's hands.

FINCHES have short beaks shaped like triangles for cracking open seeds. They make nests in trees and bushes. Male finches, with their red or yellow coloring, are brighter than female finches.

CROWS eat most anything, from berries to earthworms . . . even garbage. They line their twig nests with soft materials such as fur and moss. Crows are among the smartest animals on Earth, using and sometimes making tools and solving puzzles.

GEESE eat a variety of grasses and berries. They nest on the ground in places where they can see predators. Geese work together, flying in groups, taking turns leading the way at the front of a V formation.

EAGLES soar the skies alone, and with their hooked beaks, they hunt for fish and mammals to eat. At five to six feet across, eagle nests are among the largest of bird nests. Bald eagles are not really bald—they have white-feathered heads.

GULLS eat many foods, including clams, fish, and trash. They usually live near water, digging shallow holes for nesting and lining these nests with leaves and other soft matter. Gulls are loud, and sometimes sound like they are laughing.

HAWKS soar through the sky, seeking small animals to eat. They perch and nest in tall trees, on cliff edges, or on poles with good views. Hawks have excellent eyesight, and some can dive for prey at over 100 miles per hour.

JAYS eat mainly seeds and nuts, and sometimes they eat insects. Using sticks, they build bowl-shaped nests in trees. Jays are noisy and will chase away bigger birds, such as hawks and owls, by calling to and flying after them.

HERONS have long pointy bills for spearing fish. They build twig and leaf nests high up in trees, often with many other herons, in nesting grounds called rookeries. The wingspan of a great blue heron is as wide as an average adult human is tall.

MOCKINGBIRDS eat insects in summer and fruit and nuts in winter. Males build the outsides of nests, and females line the insides. Northern mockingbirds have a white patch on each wing and can imitate the calls of many other birds.

HUMMINGBIRDS use their long, thin beaks and tongues to drink flower nectar. The smallest birds on Earth, they can make nests from cotton, plants, dryer lint, and soft grasses. When hummingbirds hover, their wings make humming sounds.

NUTHATCHES hop up and down trees, eating insects they find in tree bark. They also stuff nuts and seeds into bark and break them with their beaks. Nuthatches build nests in tree holes. They often walk down trees headfirst.

ORIOLES eat nectar, insects, and fruit. To stay safe from predators, female orioles hang their nests, woven with grass and hair, from trees. Orioles like oranges, and many people attract orioles to their yards with cut orange halves.

ROBINS eat earthworms, insects, and fruit. They build nests made from mud, twigs, and grass and puff their feathers up to stay warm when it is chilly. Female American robins lay bright blue eggs.

OWLS have fringe-tipped feathers to help them silently swoop down on prey. They are nighttime creatures, usually spending their days sleeping in tree holes or on hidden branches. Owls can turn their heads almost all the way around.

SPARROWS eat seeds and insects. They live in grassy fields, lawns, and gardens, building nests in trees, birdhouses, and even holes in buildings. Sparrows have rounded heads and are most often brown, gray, white, and black.

PIGEONS eat seeds, fruit, and food that people offer or leave behind. They live in country and city, nesting on cliff or building ledges and reusing nests from year to year. Pigeons are famous for finding their way home, and some have been trained to carry messages for people.

WOODPECKERS have strong tails for balancing on trees and long beaks for finding insects under bark. They dig holes out of tree trunks and live inside. Woodpeckers make drumming sounds with their beaks to attract mates and to say, "This territory is mine!"

FOR MARK, THE BIRD LOVER I LOVE
—A. L. V.

FOR MANDY, FOR EVERYTHING
—D. M.

If you would like to learn more about the birds that live in your area, here are a few places to begin:
BirdNote: www.birdnote.org
Cornell Lab of Ornithology: www.birds.cornell.edu
National Audubon Society: www.audubon.org
National Wildlife Federation, Garden for Wildlife Page:
www.nwf.org/How-to-Help/Garden-for-Wildlife/Create-a-Habitat.aspx
Peterson Field Guide to Birds of North America, by Roger Tory Peterson, 2008
Roger Tory Peterson Institute of Natural History: www.rtpi.org
The Sibley Guide to Birds, Second Edition, by David Allen Sibley, 2014

Library of Congress Cataloging-in-Publication Data Available

ISBN 978-0-545-69980-8
10 9 8 7 6 5 4 3 2 1   16 17 18 19 20

Printed in Malaysia   108
First edition, March 2016

The text type was set in Adobe Garamond Pro.
The display type was set in BadTyp.
The illustrations were composed with precisely cut colored and textured papers and then carefully layered.
Book design by Marijka Kostiw